THE DANCER
LA BAILARINA
ダンサー(踊り子)

by Fred Burstein
illustrated by Joan Auclair

Bradbury Press   New York
Maxwell Macmillan Canada   Toronto
Maxwell Macmillan International
New York   Oxford   Singapore   Sydney

Translation and phonetics provided and verified by Berlitz Translation Services

Bradbury Press
Macmillan Publishing Company
866 Third Avenue
New York, NY 10022

Maxwell Macmillan Canada, Inc.
1200 Eglinton Avenue East
Suite 200
Don Mills, Ontario M3C 3N1

Macmillan Publishing Company is part of the Maxwell Communication
Group of Companies.
First edition
Printed and bound in the United States of America on recycled paper.
10 9 8 7 6 5 4 3 2 1
The illustrations are rendered in pastel.
Book design by Julie Quan

LIBRARY OF CONGRESS CATALOGING-IN-PUBLICATION DATA
Burstein, Fred.
The dancer / by Fred Burstein ; illustrated by Joan Auclair.
p.   cm.
Summary: A little girl and her father walk through the city on the
way to her ballet class. Brief text in English, Spanish, and
Japanese.
ISBN 0-02-715625-7
[1. Parent and child—Fiction.   2. Interracial marriage—Fiction.
3. City and town life—Fiction.   4. Polyglot materials.]
I. Auclair, Joan, ill.   II. Title.
PZ7.B945534Dan   1993
[E]—dc20   91-41429

Good-bye, Mommy.

Hasta pronto, Mami.

(AH-sta PRON-to, MAH-mee.)

ママ、いってきます。

(MA-ma, IT-te ki-MAS.)

Good-bye, Ballerina.

Adiós, mi bailarina.

(ah-dee-OS, mi by-lah-REE-na.)

いってらっしゃい、バレリーナ。

(IT-te las-SHA-i, ba-re-RI-na.)

Hello!

¡Hola!

(¡OH-la!)

こんにちは！

(kon-NI-chi-wah!)

Smile!

¡Sonríe!

(¡sohn-REE-ay!)

チーズ！

(cheez!)

A horse.

Un caballo.

(un cah-BAH-yo.)

馬。

(u-MA.)

Beautiful!

¡Qué belleza!

(¡kay bay-YAY-sah!)

きれいね。

(KI-le-i ne.)

Flowers.

Flores.

(FLO-ray-s.)

花。

(ha-NA.)

A boat.

Una lancha.

(U-na LAHN-cha.)

ボート。

(BO-to.)

Fish.

Peces.

(PEH-say-s.)

おさかな。

(oh-SA-ka-na.)

Thank you.

Gracias.

(GRAH-see-ahs.)

ありがとう。

(a-ri-GA-to.)

My school.

Mi academia.

(mee ah-kah-DAY-mee-ah.)

わたしの学校。

(wa-TA-shi no gak-KO.)

My friends.

Mis amigas.

(mees ah-MEE-gahs.)

わたしのともだち。

(wa TA-shi no to-mo-DA-chi.)

Good-bye, Daddy.

Adiós, Papi.

(ah-dee-OS, PAH-pee.)

パパ、バイバイ。

(PA-pa, bai-bai.)

Begin.

A comenzar.

(ah koh-men-SAHR.)

始まりまーす。

(ha-ji-MA-ri MAHS.)